GRANDMA'S
HOUSE OF
RULES

By Henry Blackshaw

Mum is taking me to Grandma's house.
I love Grandma, but jeez… she has a lot of rules.

Grandma has rules for every room. Like in the living room...

"Don't move the porcelain dogs!"

"Don't leave your toys on the floor!"

"Don't forget to plump the cushions!"

There are some rules I understand.

"Don't use the table without the tablecloth!"

"Don't do anything messy without wearing an apron!"

Then there are others that are just plain weird.

"Don't sit on the special chair. It's just for looking at!"

"Don't eat fruit with your hands!"

I could be sitting doing nothing and I'd still be breaking a rule.

Don't put your elbows on the table!

Don't put a drink down without a mat!

There is one rule that is more important than all the others.
Don't ever, *ever* touch the big blue and white vase!

The vase is older than Grandma. Our family has owned it
for longer than anyone can remember.

I once asked Grandma, "Why so many rules?"
She looked a bit confused, then replied,
"I've been following them my whole life, Kid.
I learned the rules from my grandma and she learned
them from her grandma…

…I can't start breaking them now."

So Grandma is popping to the shops.
On the way out she says, "Be good Kid,
just remember those few rules."

Rules, rules, rules…
I just have to remember the rules.

Hmm, what should I do? I know, I'll have a snack.
That will keep me out of trouble.

Don't worry, when I've finished
I won't leave my dirty plate on the table!

Now, how about playing this game of Grandma's...

Oh jeez...

Just can't reach it…

Got it!

Phew!

CREAK

Ok, don't panic. Where does Grandma keep the glue?

Now, what did Grandma say about wearing
an apron and working at the table?

This is no good.
I just can't get it right.

How about
this?

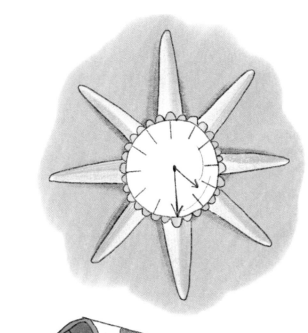

Or maybe this?

I'm not sure about this!

Nothing is going right!

Oh jeez!

Grandma takes a deep breath and then says, "It's... It's ok, Kid... it really is.

In fact, it's nice to have a few of your toys out.

Plus, the porcelain dogs look good like that."

Then Grandma puts her arm around me and and gives me the biggest hug she has given me in a long time.

"You can break a vase, Kid...

...but you could never
break my heart."

Grandma's House of Rules

Text and illustration © Henry
Blackshaw

The moral right of the author has
been asserted

British Library Cataloguing-in-
Publication Data.

A CIP record for this book is available
from the British Library
ISBN: 978-1-908714-93-0
First published in the UK, 2021 and
in the USA, 2022

Printed in Poland

CO
Cicada Books Ltd
48 Burghley Road
London NW5 1UE
www.cicadabooks.co.uk